CHRISTOPHER OCHEJA

THE BATTLE OF OTUKPO

Dedicated to the best mother to walk the earth, Mrs. Priscilla Alolo Ocheja. I love you.

"You mean so much to me, Iveh. I've never been a romantic, and I have never had the words to tell a woman how I feel but I hope these words make my feelings for you abundantly clear; Neither gods nor men would compel me to let another man have you, I would burn down villages and tear down every dwelling in them before I let any man take you away from me. I will wage war against gods and men for your heart, Iveh. I swear by every god of every Kingdom known to man…"

-King Terkura

Contents

Preface

The events of this title take place before the raid of Ojuwo Ubomu.

Acknowledgement

Much love to my family, the wolf pack, my check and navy blue brothers, my friends around the globe, and those lovely people all over the world who have my back. Thank you all so much. Bless your hearts.

Sen. Dangana Emmanuel Ocheja, Mrs.Priscilla Alolo Ocheja, Talatu Ojounugwa Ocheja, Peter Ainoko Ocheja, Joseph Idachaba Ocheja, Maria Ojochide Ocheja, Juliet Ugbedeojo Ocheja, Mr. Nuhu Bello, Mr. Adejoh Jibrin, Aunt Laraba Ocheja, Aunt Maimuna, Mr. Haruna Ocheja, Mr. Usman Ocheja, Mrs. Macaulay, Mr. Musa Honorable, Uncle Thomas Duniya, Isayas Teklay, Philip 'Dwyane' Egbuagu, Filmon 'Tough Juice' Zewengel, Johnson 'Gigante' Ojofu, Yemi Victor Adesoba, Seun Isaac Oladele, Franklin Tukura Udegbe, Festus Mvkamv Udegbe, Stephen Obekpa, Austin Chibuzor Ezeihuaku, Kenneth Giwa, Femi Oseya, Solomon Akinmoluwa, Michael Akinmoluwa, Paul Anyankpele, Tope Jones, Peter Shy Oyakhire, Jideofor 'JDX' Ezendu, Chuka 'Smiles' Ndife, Ifeanyi 'Ipocs' Okpala, Philip Jego, Oche Charles Edachie, Jude 'Cino' Okafor, Aondogu Raymond Gbajime, Martins Bobo Adeyemi, Emeka Agbai, Chijioke 'CJ' Uchendu, Cyrus Ebiloma, Chuka Enekebe, John Ahom, Okezie Nwoka, Izunna Uzokwe, Obinna Muoka, Johnson Chukwuma Ahuruonye, Robert Umoette, Terkura Waya, Chibuzor Dante Onwe, Kolapo Agunbiade, Gbolahon Agunbiade,

Ifeanyi Ike, Omale Omoha, Dozie Emechebe, Kelechi Osigwe, Henry Ibekie, Joseph Adaji, Maxwell Okpala, Adams 'Arcade' Adagiri, Chidubem Ononuju, Chinedu Ononuju, Obiora .N. Obi, Obiora .A. Obi, Nwanise Etienam, Anthony Ozovehe, Gerald Umoru, Yomi Ippinaiye, Chiedozie Hector Okoro, Douglas Dominic Obi, Victor Uchuno, Collins Caleb Zagni, Valentine Arokoyo, Torkuma Zendesha, Segun Alonge, Duke Eli Gamaliel, Helyuda Gaya Adanaya, Abraham 'Harrod Gavi' Jatau, Micah Shikaan, Charles Ihenyen, Samuel Adagba, Peter Sesugh Gundu, Abdul 'Jin Kazama' Umar, Paul Dipe, Yomi 'Yayo' Ahmed, Kelsey Dappa, Michael Elekpa, Mohammed 'Mo' Abdul, Tunji Olaleye, Güney Koçyiğit, Rahama John, Lehem Alazar, Nosa Imasuen, Aesosa Ogunbor, Enina Nelson, Kemal Karaduman, Çağatay Güven, Kitipak 'X' Phromthatri, Hassan Fikir, Erman Korbay, Claude Fany Tchoupe, Moses 'Shadow Moses' Adeyemi, Umar Lawal, Ismail Mohammed Adams, Mimi, Sixtus Daudu, Elena 'Pa!' Ambaba, Nete Otuokon, Johnson 'Jay' Egbuniwe, Adonis 'Obazzzrrrr' Obaze, Mayowa Malik Ashafa, Segun 'Sucre' Samson, Moses Adolor, Martins Adolor, The lovely people at Reedsy, Kano state, the city of Abuja, Kogi State, the state of Alaska, the city of Los Angeles, every CKC student past and present, Türkiye, Kuzey Kıbrıs Türk Cumhuriyeti, The lovely people at Gloria Jeans Coffees, everyone of my former classmates from Abang to Zendesha, and everyone who helped make me the man that I am today. The rising tide raises all ships; I rise, you rise. I wish you all good fortune through the years to come. I appreciate you all. **THE STRENGTH OF THE PACK IS THE WOLF AND THE STRENGTH OF THE WOLF IS THE PACK.**

To those who've journeyed to the afterlife to watch over us from the spiritual realm, Pascal Ibekie, Japhet Shaapera, Paul Jarumi, Emuobome Okpalaefe, Lanre Oseya, Alfred Shetima, Stanley Eteimo, Aunt Joy Sunday, Aminu Ocheja, and my maternal and paternal grand parents, it was an honor. Love and miss you all.

1

SILVER-TONGUED BEAUTY

It had for some time been anticipated by those in the know; the day the Idoma and Tiv Kings would finally meet on the battlefield. Once good friends, brothers even, the bond between the two Kings would take a terrible turn. Their friendship was brought to a sudden end by what most would call every man's weakness; a woman. Okpoju, the Idoma King, was a known womanizer, as was his friend, King Terkura of the Tiv tribe. Both married with eight and twelve children respectively, and with two beautiful wives, the two Kings could not help themselves when their gaze fell on a beautiful woman; they had to have her. Their love for women was one of the things that built their strong friendship, and unfortunately, it was also the very thing that came to cause the deep hatred between them.

Love was a thing both Okpoju and Terkura reserved only for their wives. Though they slept with countless women across many lands, their love for their wives was without question. Through decades of womanizing, neither King had ever as much as had the thought of committing to another woman, until now. Her name was Iveh, a stunning, soft-spoken, silver-tongued beauty men were willing to do unspeakable things to other men for. Her eyes were a bright light brown, and looking into them was like being pulled into a bottomless pit from which there was no escape. Her hourglass figure made the faint of heart tremble in front of their wives at the sight of her, visibly battling not to stare, which was often a wasted effort; they gave in eventually. When Iveh spoke, men stood still and listened with undivided attention. They gave in to her will with no questions asked, no hesitation. Iveh knew her worth, she knew the effect she had on men, and she knew very well how to use it.

It was on a day the Tiv were celebrating another year of the King's reign. Performers of all kinds put on their best to entertain King Terkura and the crowd. From one good performance garnering applause to another, the day was filled with mind-blowing entertainment. After several such performances, a woman walked her way slowly onto the arena. With each step she took, the crowd of predominantly men quieted down more and more until most of the men present were completely silent.

Kings Terkura and Okpoju were laughing and high-fiving each other when they noticed the young woman approaching. The grins faded from their faces, and their eyes followed her as she walked.

The Kings and crowd of men ogled the beauty until she got to the centre of the arena, bowed her head, and said the words, "Good morning, my Kings. I am honored to have been given the chance to perform for Your Highness. I shall speak of the day until I am grey and need the aid of a cane to walk," King Okpoju grinned sheepishly, blushing, "As all can see, I have nothing in hand. I cannot play the drums like our fine drummers, or do flips like our great acrobats, no one can dance like our masquerades, but the gods have granted me the gift of a song. I hope it pleases the crowd and Your Highness."

She spoke with such calmness and humility the crowd adored her. They let out a subtle "Oooh," at the gracious way she ended her speech.

She cleared her throat, the King's leaned further from their seats, and Iveh uttered her first notes. Her voice was so gentle yet so powerful. Both kings looked at each other in disbelief, eyes in the crowd spelt astonishment, and women whose husbands were caught by Iveh's spell reeked of envy. Iveh sang her way into the heads and hearts of thousands of men that day, and none more than Kings Okpoju and Terkura. In their heads, both Kings drifted into their fantasies; Okpoju's was of him leading Iveh through a garden of beautiful green plants, and Terkura's was of him and Iveh taking their vows and starting a family. They basked in their fantasies through the duration of Iveh's song and were only brought back to reality when it ended. When it was over, the crowd broke into loud, energetic applause. Men rose to their feet, clapping enthusiastically, as did the Kings. Iveh stood in the middle of it all with her head tilted and a subtly-bright smile on her face. Even many of the envious women couldn't help but join in the applause, Iveh's voice was angelic. King Okpoju waved his hands, gesturing the crowd to quiet down. When the place was quiet enough, the King cleared his throat.

"That was wonderful! That is the best song I have ever heard in all my days. Young lady, what is your name?"

"I am Iveh Ahom, Your Highness."

"Wonderful. Iveh Ahom, I think I speak for most men here when I say I can listen to you sing every day for the rest of my life," King Terkura said, gesturing to the crowd.

The men agreed with the King, some nodding and others

saying, "Yes," and "Oh, yes."

"You are by far my favorite performer of the day, and for that, you will have twenty bags of grain and a hundred gold coins to your name!"

The crowd applauded the King's generosity. King Okpoju eyed King Terkura, he knew where this was going, and he was going to beat him there, whatever it took. "Indeed, and my gift to you, thirty bags of grain and a hundred and fifty gold coins," the Idoma King added.

The crowd cheered King Okpoju, but some had quizzical looks on their faces as they wondered what was going on; it seemed to them the Kings were in competition.

King Terkura looked over at his friend, a bit confused, but smiled as he continued, "Yes, very generous. Iveh, your voice has brought you so much this day, and that is not all. I was going to ask if you had enough room in your dwelling for a colt?"

"Well, Your Highness, room can be made," Iveh replied.

"Then it is finished. Have the finest colt in my stable delivered to her dwelling immediately," King Terkura said, gesturing to his warriors.

King Okpoju had every intention and the means to match the Tiv King's gift but thought it would make things too obvious, so he relented, smiled, and clapped for the King instead.

"Thank you, Your Highness. You have given this common girl from Gboko so much. I don't know that I deserve this much."

"Ohhh," the crowd responded, clapping yet again.

King Terkura saw how much the crowd was drawn to her. In his head, he imagined how she'd be a perfect fit as Queen.

Iveh exited the floor, making room for the next performer, a magician. The magician's tricks were quite impressive, but King Terkura's mind was far from the arena. His mind had room for little else besides Iveh. King Okpoju couldn't stop thinking about her either, so he came up with a clever Idea. Knowing Terkura was bound by honor and duty to sit through the celebration, he excused himself, telling his friend, "I'm pressed, brother. I must go and ease myself. You Tiv, your great cuisine will do that to a man," and both King's shared a laugh. Okpoju left in search of Iveh, through a crowd of spectators, and then through a smaller crowd of performers until he saw her at a distance walking into her tent.

Iveh was stood in front of a mirror humming so beautifully the King was about to say words but refrained to savor the moment. She hummed for a while until she noticed the King in her mirror. Startled, she turned her gaze to him.

"Your Highness, forgive me. I didn't notice you there," she said, about to kneel.

"No, no....it is I who must apologise. It was rude of me to come in unannounced. Please rise," said King Okpoju, gesturing, "You have an extraordinary voice."

"Thank you, Your Highness," said Iveh with her eyes shifting from side-to-side, obviously wondering why the King was in her tent.

"I thought I'd come by and know more about the woman who might've given me the best song of my life. Tell me, Iveh, are you spoken for?"

"Spoken for? Your Highness, I don't understand what y...."

"I mean do you have a man in your life, a husband?"

"Oh, forgive me, Your Highness. I am not familiar with the parlance. No, the gods have not seen it fit to bless me with a man yet."

"Hmmm, maybe they have been saving you for the right one; a man who can tend to your every need and take proper care of you. Maybe he is stood right here in front of you," the King said, opening his arms, presenting himself as though the greatest gift.

Iveh smiled knowing where the King was going but played coy, "I don't understand, Your Highness."

"I am saying, it'll be my honor to be that man for you, or at least, to be given a chance to prove that I can be that man."

"I have never been sought after by a King before. I don't know what to say, Your Highness."

"Say you will give me a chance. I know a girl like you must've been chased by men for as long as you've used your legs to walk. Give me the chance to show you what none of them possibly could," King Okpoju asserted.

"Well, your grace, since you put it that way, a common girl like me dare not say no. I am flattered."

"So you'll give me a chance?"

"Yes, Your Highness, a chance, I suppose it couldn't hurt."

"Well then," King Okpoju said happily, clapping his hands. "You have made me a very happy man today. You will not regret that decision. Okpoju gives his word. My guards will deliver everything I promised to you. Until we meet again, Iveh," he said, before leaving the tent.

When he left, Iveh looked at her reflection in the mirror, a smile crept onto her face; she had a King caught in her web, and she knew it.

The celebration had ended, most had left the arena, and Iveh was riding out, escorted by some of Okpoju's men when she heard horses galloping towards her and a voice calling out, "Iveh, wait, a moment please." It was King Terkura and two of his guards. Iveh stopped her horse, the King rode to her, came off his horse, and walked over saying, "Iveh, walk with me for a moment please," taking her hand, helping her off her horse. Iveh climbed down and walked with King Terkura, further and further away from the ears and eyes of the guards. The look of things made Terkura and Okpoju's men look to each other confused as the King and Iveh faded into the darkening night.

"If I didn't have an audience with you, a good night's sleep would have been impossible for a while."

"Oh, My King, your words warm the heart."

"It is you who warms the heart, my dear. I am a man who believes in transparency and honesty. I won't bore you with clever lines, insult your intellect with scattered wits, or waste your time by beating around the bush. I know you know why a man like me would ride after a woman like you, and I know a woman like you has countless suitors, so let me go straight to it and promise you that amongst all of those many men seeking your hand, not one of them will do what Terkura would do for you. Whatever your heart desires will be yours, you need only utter the words and have them fall on my ears, and Terkura will have whatever you desire at your feet. If you were mine, you would have my heart and the entire Kingdom as your playground. I would roam the streets with an empty hole in my chest, unable to fall for any other woman, for my heart would be in your possession. Now that you have heard me say the words and know how I feel, what say you?" said King Terkura, stopping and facing Iveh.

"My King, there are no words for how honored I am to be sought after by you, but another has only recently asked for my hand."

"In marriage?"

"No, Your Highness, he asked for a chance to win my heart."

"Well, not to force your decision, but I am sure whoever he is, he is not a King, and even if he was, he is not Terkura of the Tiv tribe. Your choice is an easy one the way I see it."

"This might be true, Your Highness, but I already agreed to it."

King Terkura laughs. "I never thought I'd be fighting a common man for a woman's heart, but if I were to do so for any woman in the world it'd be you. So Iveh, since this man is not your husband and from what I can tell you are not bound by any sacred oath, perhaps you could give me the chance you are giving him and let me prove myself?"

Iveh thought about it. "Alright, Your Highness. I suppose that's fair."

"Iveh, may the gods see you to your dwelling safe, and grant you the gift of a good night's sleep. I will be seeing you again, before long."

"Thank you, Your Highness. Have a goodnight."

2

BEST-KEPT SECRET

For the better part of the next six months, the Kings went to lengths they hadn't ever before, trying to win Iveh's heart. They did things they never did for any other woman prior, not even their wives.

King Terkura spoiled her with extravagant gifts like the gifts of a massive dwelling, livestock, farming land, the best clothing his Kingdom had to offer, and more. When Iveh needed his attention, he ordered everyone and everything postponed for her. Once, she'd feared she caught an infection from a cut she suffered while cooking, and King Terkura summoned the best herbalist in the land to treat her. When he found Iveh was fine, for preventing such an occurrence in the future the King got her a cook so she never had to be in the kitchen again. There was also a day when Iveh was trying to practice her singing, and the noise of nearby masons wouldn't let her hear herself, so the King ordered all the masons within fifty kilometres to seize work for a fortnight.

King Okpoju bought her gifts as well, but the Idoma King was also very romantic. He did the little things like remembering how many sennights had gone by since they'd met, notice how Iveh ate fish and chicken but avoided beef, how she looked to the ground whenever she was paid a compliment, and how her eyelids were naturally darker than usual. He noticed she cared deeply for her little brother, and he'd often buy him gifts, ask about him, and even befriended him over time. Okpoju made the little boy laugh a lot with his jokes and antics. The bond he'd built with her little brother was making Iveh fall more for him than she was for Terkura. Both men were unique individuals with singular personalities but Okpoju's might've been working better for Iveh; his clumsiness around her, his comical arrogance, the way he often spoke of himself in the third person, and the countless interesting stories he never failed to tell. Terkura was a bit more uptight, a man of fewer words who cared way more about status, reputation, and the impression he gave people in general. Underneath it all, however, Iveh could see Terkura's genuine love for her and how he would bend and break to make her happy. She knew without question when it came down to it, reputation, status, and everything else would be pushed aside for her sake, and for that, she had a soft spot in her heart for him.

For six months Iveh was Terkura and Okpoju's best-kept secret from one another. Neither of them felt comfortable telling the other they'd gone after her knowing very well how they were drawn to her the first time they saw her. They met often, as usual, they discussed everything but recently they hadn't been discussing women as much, not at all really.

After hours of one of such meetings, Terkura would notice this new change and ask his friend, "Okpoju, you haven't mentioned anything about your women lately, is everything alright?"

"All is well, brother. Okpoju has his eyes on better things. That's all."

"Better things than the company of beautiful women? What has become of my friend?"

Okpoju giggled. "Nothing has happened to me, my friend. I still like the company of a beautiful woman, but I have decided my days of chasing them across lands far and wide have come to an end. I have eyes only for one now."

"By the gods! I never thought I'd see the day those words would fall from those lips. Blessings, my friend. May the gods bless your union with your wife. It's no surprise you are giving up all your women for her. I always knew your love for her was... .."

"It's not my wife," Okpoju said, cutting Terkura off.

"Not your wife? Brother, another woman won your heart? I never thought I'd live to see that either. Who is she? What tribe? Is she Idoma, Tiv, Igala, Yoruba? Wait.....there have been rumors about you coming to my Kingdom and sneaking in and out of places. She must be a Tiv girl. Tell me, brother."

"Okpoju shall keep this one a secret, even from you, brother."

"Alright, my friend, I understand. You don't have to tell me who she is. I must confess I have eyes for one as well. You know how much I love my wife, and I always will until the day the sun and moon no longer grace the sky, but this girl is different. Something about her makes me feel my life would be incomplete until she takes the vow and she is mine."

"The gods are wonderful indeed, who would've thought the great King Terkura would utter words so romantic about any woman at all, talk more of one who isn't his wife? Do you care to share her name?"

"Do you think me foolish, brother? You refused to give your

woman's name, and you sit there asking me of mine? You must've lost your mind."

King Okpoju laughed hysterically. "A man can try. It is alright, my friend, you don't have to tell me," He exhaled, giggled for a moment, shaking his head in thought, "The gods have their ways. They do indeed. Okpoju and Terkura married about the same time, had children at about the same time, chased and bedded countless women together for many years, and now here we are speaking of finding love outside of marriage at the same time. It seems, brother, we might have the same blessing or curse from the gods."

Terkura nodded his head in agreement, thinking of his friend's statement.

"Here's to true love, friendship, and mercy from the gods," Okpoju said, pouring a bit of his drink on the floor.

"To true love, friendship, and mercy," King Terkura responded, pouring his drink.

The Kings parted shortly after, jolly and bubbly at first, but as the hours went by, both men felt strange about their exchange; they wondered who their love interests were, where she was from, the timing, and the thought even crept in that they might've been chasing the same woman.

"Iveh spoke of another man, could it have been Okpoju? No, It couldn't be," King Terkura wondered.

"Is it at all possible Terkura and I are going after the same woman? No, that would be too great a coincidence; you have a better chance of rain in the harmattan season than that. Besides, if there was another man Iveh would tell me, wouldn't she?" King Okpoju pondered.

On the day of the ceremony, they'd both left feeling they got to her first. Okpoju assumed since he'd gotten to her before his friend had the chance Iveh would be decent enough to turn down anyone else's advances. Terkura believed Okpoju never got the chance to go after Iveh during the ceremony. From what he could remember, he was seated next to him the whole time. He also assumed it was a common man he was competing against to win Iveh's heart, and he was confident he'd come out the victor.

The thought of the possibility of them falling for the same woman kept hammering in their heads, their spirits grew uneasy, and both men wanted closure, so they decided to keep a close eye on one another, tasking their best spies to find out who the other's love interest was. The way they saw it, chances were it wouldn't be the same woman, and they'd move on with their lives without feeling the guilt of betraying their friendship by spying on each other.

After a fortnight of watching each other in the shadows, Terkura's spy gave him the news, and the King launched at him, furious, as he said, "Silence! It cannot be. Okpoju would never! I thought you were supposed to be the best spy in the Kingdom?"

"I am, Your Highness, it is as I have said. I swear it by the gods," the spy managed to say through gnashed teeth, with his hands in the air, and the King's wrapped around his neck.

King Terkura released the spy and walked to the corner of his throne room. "How could this have happened? Is this how the gods have chosen to punish us for our years of womanizing? How can my brother and I fall for the same woman?" the King said, baffled and utterly confused.

In Otukpo, King Okpoju's spy revealed to him who it was, and the King had a similar reaction. He got up, drew his sword, and said, "You would watch your tongue, or Okpoju would part it from your lips."

"Your Highness, I have done this for thirty years, and I have never been wrong. On my life, I know I am right," the spy said, kneeling and bowing before his King.

King Okpoju threw his sword on the ground, looked up as if to the gods above, and said the words, "Is this how you have chosen to punish us? My brother and I, the same woman?"

For days the King's sat in the quiet of their chambers, attempting to drink their sorrows away. After days of much thought, Okpoju decided, "I have never felt this way in my life, I cannot let her go, not even for Terkura," and King Terkura decided, "Forgive me, brother, not even the gods can compel me to leave Iveh."

King Okpoju rode to Iveh's dwelling the following night to hear what she had to say. When she saw him climbing off his horse, she hurried over and embraced him, but the Idoma King didn't appear to share her enthusiasm. Noticing this, Iveh asked, "What is the matter, My King?"

"Iveh, Okpoju bears a heavy burden in his heart. I have a question to ask you, and I want you to be honest with me."

"What is it? Go on, ask me anything."

"Is there another man in your life besides me?"

Iveh was taken by the King's question. She looked away, took a few steps towards space across from them. "Yes, my King. I didn't know how, when, or if I should tell you. I wanted to, but I feared what it might do to us, or both of you."

"So it is true, you have been seeing me and my closest friend, my brother?" said Okpoju, fighting his emotions.

"It wasn't what I intended. That day you both asked for a chance. I didn't know how to reject a King. I thought no harm could come from it. I was sure I'd know who the right man was and part with the other, but then, in your unique ways, you won my heart. The longer I kept seeing you, the deeper I fell for both of you. I've never been cared for as you've both cared for me. I've never been as happy."

"So, you love him?"

"Yes, I do. But I also love you. I can't find the words to explain. You are both special to me. You both have your ways of brightening my day. Every moment with both of you means so much."

"When did this even happen? When did he ask you for your hand?"

"After the ceremony, hours after you came to my tent."

"Iveh, when I am away from you, it feels like I am shackled and in a prison where the walls are made of anguish, the floor is made of pain and the bars of melancholy. Each moment away from you feels like you are slipping out of my grasp. What I feel for you cannot yet be put into words. I want you to be mine and mine alone. I cannot share you with another man," he shook his head momentarily, "I cannot share you with anyone. You have to decide. You must decide who you love more, is it me or him? Whatever your decision, I will try to live with it. If you say yes, Okpoju would be the happiest man dead or living, and if you say no, I do not know what would become of me, but I will try to accept that decision."

Iveh stood quietly, unable to find the words to answer.

"The next time you see me, I hope you have an answer. Decide, Iveh, decide," King Okpoju said, mounting his horse and riding away.

About a sennight later, Terkura would have a sit-down of his own with Iveh.

"So, my friend was the other man? You must think a goddess of yourself, toying with the hearts of Kings."

"Don't be like that, my King. That wasn't my intention."

"Then what was your intention, Iveh? To have us both pour our hearts to you and then dump one of us in the end without care for what it might do to us? You knew he was my closest friend. Why didn't you tell me from the start?"

"My King, I got so confused, and you were both so good to me and...."

"Oh, stop! You only cared about yourself from the beginning. You didn't care what any of this did to any of us. If you did, you would've had the courtesy to at least tell one of us the man on the other side was a dear friend."

"That's not true," Iveh said with her hands over her mouth, starting to shed tears.

"No, no, no, don't cry. I'm sorry, Iveh," said King Terkura, embracing her. "You mean so much to me, Iveh. I've never been a romantic, and I have never had the words to tell a woman how I feel but I hope these words make my feelings for you abundantly clear; Neither gods nor men would compel me to let another man have you, I would burn down villages and tear down every dwelling in them before I let any man take you away from me. I will wage war against gods and men for your heart, Iveh. I swear by every god of every Kingdom known to man. Do you hear me, Iveh? I will wage war."

Locked in his embrace, Iveh had a worrisome look on her face; she found the King's words subtly romantic yet really frightening.

At another one of their regularly scheduled meetings, Okpoju and Terkura would come face to face for the first time in a while. Seated in Okpoju's throne room, the two friends who usually had much to laugh and shake hands about barely had any words for each other. The hammering of working men and sparring warriors outside echoed through the room as both men sat in silence, looking everywhere other than each other's eyes. The obvious elephant in the room needed to be addressed, but neither King would start the conversation. After a long period of awkward silence, Okpoju had enough.

"Oh, by the gods, brother! Let's address the obvious and be done with it. I know you are the other man after Iveh's heart, and I'm sure you know about me and her."

"Of course I do, and it is out of the love I have for you that I did not ride here with more of my warriors to take your head," said King Terkura.

"How did you find out about us?" said Okpoju, leaning forward with curiosity in his eyes.

"The same way I'm sure you did, my friend. And don't even try to tell me otherwise, I know you too well."

"There is no denying it, I am guilty as charged. I had you followed."

"So much for our friendship, one whiff of a pretty girl and we throw the sanctity of our brotherhood into the latrine pit."

"You and I are more than friends, we are brothers. It is almost abominable what is happening here. Please, one of us has to let her go before the gods rain worse curses on us."

"I agree with you, my brother. That is why I think you should let her go."

"Terkura, you and your arrogance, and why should I be the one who relents?"

"Because amongst other things, I am the older of both us, only by a full moon, but older still, and Iveh came to my ceremony to perform for me, and you knew very well what my intentions were, but you tried to be clever and snuck into her tent, claiming you had to ease yourself. Did you think I wouldn't put that together? I remember how you gave her more of the very gifts I gave her so that you could buy yourself a step ahead of me. Your betrayal of me started the moment you saw me make the move on her," King Terkura said, getting angry.

"Nonsense! We both saw her, we both wanted her, and we both went after her not knowing the other was doing the same thing. Did I try to do better than you to impress her? Yes, I did, but since when was that an issue between you and me? We have done that many times with many women over the years. Why does it upset you now all of a sudden? I didn't betray you, my friend. I fell for her the same as you."

"So, what are you saying, brother? Are you refusing to let her go?"

"Why wouldn't you, Terkura? You claim to be the older of us both, act like it, give us your blessing, and let us be."

"Brother, I said this to Iveh, and I am going to say it to you right now; neither gods nor men will ever compel me to let go of Iveh, not even you. I will burn down villages and tear down every dwelling before I let that happen. I love you, brother, but if you do not leave this be, you will be my enemy, and I wage war against all of my enemies."

Okpoju felt insulted by Terkura's threat. He calmly rose from his seat. "I suppose it is settled, war then," the Idoma King said walking towards the exit.

"Okpoju, don't walk away from me. If you leave this throne room, you leave as my enemy. I will take your head and burn Otukpo to the ground if you dare to try me!" King Terkura barked, fuming with rage as he watched Okpoju walking out.

King Okpoju ignored him, exited the throne room, and left the palace.

And so it began; a feud that started between two Kings and grew into a deep hatred between two Kingdoms. For the two months that followed, King Terkura prepared his warriors for an attack on Otukpo, Okpoju prepared his warriors to defend his Kingdom, and the Idoma and Tiv tribes though mostly unaware of what exactly caused the rift between their Kings were at each other's throats. Their King's spoke of the other tribe's treachery and that was reason enough for their people. Every Idoma resident on Tiv soil and vice versa got stares, name-calling, were targeted by thieves and burglars, and if you were a criminal found wanting you got the worst of whatever punishment was fitting for your crime.

Even through all of the battle preparation Terkura made time for Iveh. On a cold, quiet night he took an unescorted ride to her dwelling to ease his mind of all the stress of battle preparations.

"Iveh, I'm sure you know by now what's about to happen?"

"Yes, my King, I do," Iveh replied, wearing her sadness on her face.

"You disapprove?" King Terkura asked, noticing the look on her face.

"Of course I disapprove. You want me to be happy that you're about to kill each other?"

"So it is him you love, is that it?"

"I didn't say that, so why are you hearing it, my King? Did the two of you ever stop to think of what this could do to me? If any of you dies, it will tear me apart. And when the people find out the real reason why all of this happened, can you imagine the names they would call me in the streets? The way even children will sing songs in mockery of me?"

"Any man, woman, or child who does that will answer to me. They wouldn't dare!"

"Please, don't do this, I beg you," Iveh pleaded, kneeling and grabbing both of Terkura's hands.

"It is too late for that. I told you, I would wage war on gods and men for you, those weren't mere words, I meant it."

"So you're just going to ride into Otukpo and fight until you kill him? You were friends, brothers!"

"No brother of mine would seek the heart of a woman he knows belongs to me. It is as you said, I will ride into Otukpo and kill every weapon-wielding warrior until I get to Okpoju and take his head off his shoulders," the King said, seeing the image so vividly in his head it almost felt real. "He is preparing his warriors, but he won't see me coming, I shall go like a thief in the night, when they are snoring in bed. It will be on the last night of this sennight. That night, Okpoju's soul will be received by Alekwu."

At the mention of this Iveh's eyes swayed left to right; she had to save Okpoju.

Iveh loved Terkura, but her heart truly belonged to Okpoju. The next day, she snuck out of Gboko, and traveled to Otukpo to tell Okpoju of Terkura's plans to attack on the last night of the sennight. The Idoma King had a very capable force, but he knew his chances in an open battle against the Tor Tiv's great warriors were slim. Knowing when Terkura intended to attack increased his chances but gave him no significant advantage, so Okpoju decided it was time to call in a favor a great King owed him. The King in question was known to have one of the most lethal fighting forces in the entire world. His warriors would tip the scales in Okpoju's favor, that was certain, but this King was a man of honor and immense discipline, Okpoju would have a very difficult time convincing him to fight in a battle that was over a woman. Of course, he knew he could try lying about the real reason for the battle, but this King had many times in the past had great knowledge of the strangest things, he even seemed clairvoyant to many. Okpoju knew better than trying to play on his intelligence. That would be a risk that might cost him the war, for if this King were to spot his lie he most certainly would not be sending his men to fight.

At first light, Okpoju, Iveh, and his entourage rode through Ojuwo Ubomu, Okete aga idoko, until they were stood before the massive palace of the Atta of Igala, King Idachaba. The gates opened and stood before Okpoju and his entourage were King Idachaba, Queen Egbunu, Ngodi, and the degeli.

At the sight of the Idoma King, King Idachaba said, "When my messengers told me King Okpoju of the Idoma tribe was in my Kingdom I must admit I thought they must've been mistaken. I thought, by this time of year he's still slumbering somewhere after having drunk hundreds of barrels of Palm wine," there was a moment of silence, and then both Kings broke into laughter. "My dear friend, it's been an awfully long time. You're welcome."

"Battle-axe of Igala Mela! It is good to see you, as always," said King Okpoju, embracing Idachaba.

"I haven't been called that in a long time. Ever since...." King Idachaba stopped mid-sentence, though not showing his emotions, the memories still lingered.

"I am so sorry, my friend. I know many years have passed since, but please accept my condolences."

"Thank you, my friend."

"Ah, my Queen, your presence brightens the horizon, same as ever," King Okpoju said, tilting his head to Queen Egbunu.

"Welcome, King Okpoju. It must've been decades since we last saw you."

"It has been years, but forgive Okpoju. I admit the fault is entirely mine. As much as I would love to raise a calabash to both of you and feast through the day, I'm afraid I have very pressing matters that simply cannot wait."

"Come, my friend, tell me all about it," King Idachaba said, leading him into the palace.

Seated in the council chamber, King Idachaba and King Okpoju discussed Terkura and the battle heading to the Idoma Kingdom.

"So, you and Terkura are arming and sending thousands to battle, possibly to their deaths, over one woman's heart? A woman who knew you were friends, brothers even, and sat quietly while you were both trying to court her? The same woman heard Terkura's plans and brought them to you, knowing very well it could mean his death, you didn't find that questionable, and you've ridden here to ask me to arm and send thousands of my men to help you win your battle for this woman's heart. Okpoju, what kind of man do you think I am?" said King Idachaba.

"My friend, I know you, I know what kind of man you are, and I know how all of this looks. I swear to you, it is more complicated than that. I would never ask you to do anything dishonorable, you know that."

"You are at this very moment, my friend."

"I never wanted this war, Terkura threatened that if I do not let Iveh go I would become his enemy and he would come for me.

He is the one marching his warriors to my door steps. I am in Otukpo trying to defend my Kingdom. I am only doing my duty as King. If Terkura doesn't attack me, there would be no war. Okpoju would never march his men into Gboko to kill Terkura, he seeks to take what's mine but he is still my brother. Believe me, friend, he has gone mad."

"It saddens me to see what has become of both of you, and it pains me so, but I cannot send my men to Otukpo, not for this."

"Alright, I did not want it to come to this, my friend. I love you like a brother and you know it, but you leave me no other choice. Of all the Kings I have had the honor and privilege of knowing, you are by far the most honorable, and I know when you give your word, you keep it come hell or high water. You made me a promise all those years ago, you gave me your word, you said...."

"I know what I said, Okpoju," King Idachaba said, cutting him off.

"What then? Are you going to break your word or are you going to keep it?" Okpoju said, leaning forward, eager for the Igala King's response.

King Idachaba gave his friend a stern look of apparent displeasure. "Go back to Otukpo, Okpoju. Igala mela will defend your Kingdom."

The Idoma King thanked Idachaba and hurried out to ride back to Otukpo. Queen Egbunu walked into the council room shortly after.

"My love, you look displeased. What is it?" the Queen asked.

"Okpoju wants me to send my warriors to help defend his Kingdom. He and Terkura are going to battle over a woman."

"King Terkura, the Tor Tiv? They are brothers."

"Such is the power of a beautiful woman."

The Queen knew her husband too well. One look and she put it all together. "He reminded you of it. He used it to get you to agree," she said.

"He did."

"Some nights I have nightmares of evil spirits and all forms of monsters, but do you know which of my nightmares frighten me most, my love? The ones of war. The ones with you riding Akpai and swinging that battle-axe of yours frighten me a hundred times over. I hate war, and I hate the very thought of you being in it."

"I know. I do not like seeing what it does to you, it kills me every time. But here I am, bound by honor to ride into another one. The thought of me putting you through the pain makes me want to drop to my knees, my Queen. You know I have to keep my word."

"I know. I would never suggest you do otherwise. I under-stand, but it doesn't make it any easier."

King Idachaba held his Queen close. With his arms wrapped around her and hers around him, they shared a moment in the quiet council room.

King Okpoju rode back to Otukpo confident he had done enough to give King Terkura and his forces a hell of a fight, beat them even.

By sunset, he told his wife the truth about Iveh and revealed his intentions of marrying her. The Idoma Queen though heartbroken made her peace with the situation. Polygamy was nothing new for Kings anyway.

By nightfall, Okpoju and Iveh spoke of the battle and the risk she'd taken by betraying Terkura knowing the odds were against Okpoju. The King couldn't fall any deeper in love with her; she couldn't have done more to prove her love for him. In Okpoju's eyes, Iveh had never looked more beautiful, her voice had never been more soothing, and her figure had never been more bodacious. Everything that had brought them to this point and the thought of the endless possibilities after steered a desire in Okpoju he'd long restrained but could no longer contain. The King pulled her close, the pair looked into each other's eyes. Iveh saw his hunger for her, and he saw hers for him. In a matter of moments, the moaning and screaming of both lovers echoed through the empty corridor of the King's chamber.

3

KING TERKURA'S PLOY

In Idah, Ngodi, the warrior supreme hurried into the palace with a note his warriors had found by the gates. It carried the message, "The Tiv King rides for Otukpo. He arrives at dawn." Notes like this had been mysteriously found by the palace gates a few times over the years, and whatever information was on them always proved true. This was one of the reasons King Idachaba seemed psychic and clairvoyant to many. The King's guards never spotted the messenger; they never knew when he or she came, or where he or she came from, but experience had taught them never to take whatever message it carried for granted.

The warrior supreme delivered the message. He watched the King's eyes go wide. The King looked to the warrior supreme and told him, "Send messengers to every Chief immediately. Tell each of them to send two thousand men to the palace right away. Where are Achile and Achimugu?"

"They mentioned going to Oja Abafu's inn, Your Highness."

"Tell Odiba to go get them. Now, go!"

"Yes, Your Highness," the warrior supreme replied, bowing

and hurrying out.

King Idachaba walked into his chamber to his Queen lying in their bed. When the door opened, she sat up, noticed his demeanor, and said, "Is it time, my love?"

"Yes, my Queen."

She gave him a nod of approval. He nodded back, walked over to his battle-axe, grabs it, and grips it tightly.

At first light, a spent Okpoju woke up with a bright smile on his face and Iveh in his arms. He savored the moment, watching her sleep. His happiness would be short-lived, as soon after he heard the sounds of war horns and battle drums. Startled and confused, the King hopped out of his bed. He looked out through the window. "Iveh, wake up!" he bellowed, "Get your clothing." He hurried out of the chamber and came back with four warriors he ordered to stand by the chamber door, "Iveh, Terkura deceived us. It was a trick. He did not wait for the end of the sennight. He knew you'd tell me. How could Okpoju have been so stupid?" he said, putting both his hands over his head, pacing around the chamber, "The warriors outside will take you to a secret chamber behind the palace where you'd be safe. My wife and children would be there with four other capable warriors. If the battle seems lost they would guide you all out through the back where you can escape and get far away from here."

"But, my love....."

"There is no time, Iveh. Please go now."

Iveh sobbed as she ran out, the end to this battle under the circumstance was obvious; Okpoju was going to lose. The thought of him falling in battle would keep the tears running down her cheeks for hours.

Okpoju put on his leather armor, armed himself, and rode out to join his warriors. They stood sixty thousand strong across from Terkura's eighty thousand. When they saw their King approaching on his horse, they fixed their postures; their backs straight, chest out, and shoulders high. His presence boosted their confidence and will to fight.

"My warriors, with you Okpoju will ride into the pits of hell to face the devil himself. I will slaughter every demon in his ranks, kill the mistresses that bore them, and when I finally get to him, I will with this sword," he said drawing his sword, "Take his head off his shoulders and free men of his evil."

The warriors responded by banging their weapons to their shields and the bottom of their spears to the ground.

"Warriors, if Okpoju, your King asks you to ride with him to hell, would you follow?"

"Yes!" the warriors screamed in response.

"Then the Tiv stand no chance, think little of them. Their number is greater, and if you asked them they'd claim their warriors are the mightiest to grace the land of men, but we know better. Stand your ground and send them to their god!"

The warriors cheered their King, the horns were blowing, and the drums were beating until the King's Captain walked to him saying, "My King, he approaches," pointing at King Terkura and four others riding towards the Idoma.

The Tor Tiv rode slowly, wearing a look of anger and disgust with his eyes fixated on King Okpoju. When he got to the Idoma King his first words were, "Where is she?"

The Idoma King frowned, looking right into the Tiv King's eyes as he replied, "That is none of your concern."

The Tiv King looked through Okpoju's warriors, exhaled, and responded, "When my council suggested I tell her my plans to see what she does I almost had them all executed. I didn't question Iveh's honor or her loyalty for a moment. She made a fool out of me, but I forgive her. I don't blame her for you. I know it is you who made her do what she did. Surrender to me, ask your warriors to do the same, and I will grant you all quick deaths."

"Terkura, your breath smells of dried piss. Go lead your men, and let's finish this!"

"Gladly," King Terkura said, turning his horse and riding away.

The Tor Tiv stopped in front of his warriors. He rode from side to side looking into their eyes. Unlike Okpoju, Terkura didn't feel the need to say a lot of words, he trusted in the savagery of his men. He simply said the words, "Kill them all!" and with a hand gesture, he signalled the first attack.

The Tiv beasts needed no extra motivation to do what they do best. They charged, screaming like wild animals unleashed.

King Okpoju in response, waved his sword as he bellowed, "Archers, volley!"

The Archers let their arrows fly, killing a few Tiv.

The Tiv warriors kept running without care or fear. Even when the arrows hit and grounded some of their comrades, the warriors jumped over them and kept sprinting towards the Idoma. This was nothing new, it was the way of war and any group of warriors launching an attack would do the same, but what separated the Tiv from most was the look in their eyes; their foes could tell that in them the fear of death was non-existent. The Idoma warriors in front watched the Tiv approaching. They started beating their chests and chanting in their native tongues, reciting what their tribe believed was a battle chant that drew strength from fallen warriors of old.

"Now!" King Okpoju commanded.

The warriors on the front lines charged at the Tiv and the battle began. The muscular Tiv warriors were grabbing and body slamming the Idoma. They tossed some of them around so effortlessly it looked like they were throwing bags full of feathers. Their show of strength, though impressive, did not go unanswered by the Idoma; King Okpoju's warriors were resilient, they fell to the ground, picked themselves up, and kept fighting valiantly.

King Terkura watched the battle go on until it was time for his next attack. He raised his hand, a breath away from giving the order when he heard familiar horns and drums. With a quizzical look on his face, the King whispered, "The Igala tribe?" The ground shook as King Idachaba approached with twenty thousand of his warriors. In a matter of moments, Terkura was stood between King Idachaba's twenty thousand and Okpoju's warriors, who were now a little under sixty thousand.

King Terkura rode closer to Idachaba, stopped a distance away, as he yelled, "Gaba-Idu, you would stand against me too?"

"I have no choice, friend. I am bound."

"He held you to your promise, didn't he?"

King Idachaba nodded in response.

"Then so be it," Terkura said, about to ride back to his men.

"Wait! There is no need for further bloodshed. These men can all return to their families if you leave things be. Okpoju was your brother long before that woman meant anything to you."

"Neither gods nor men would stop me from taking that man's head. Not even you, Gaba-Idu. If you stand with him then you are my enemy and I shall send you to the afterlife along with him."

King Idachaba lacked an appreciation for threats. He nodded

his head in acceptance of Terkura's perceived challenge.

King Okpoju had a different strategy in mind before the Igala arrived. Now that they had King Terkura right in their midst, he commanded, "Full assault!" pointing ahead. All of his riders and foot warriors charged at the Tiv and both sides unleashed decimation upon each other the likes of which would haunt the dreams of any survivors this day. The savage, blood lusted Tiv and the unrelenting, resilient Idoma tribes were locked in a torrid, violent dance, bathing themselves in blood.

King Idachaba took a moment to watch the butchery, hating every second of it. The screams of all the dying men caused him great pain. The thought of the reason for it all irritated him the most, but the honorable King was bound. "Attack!" he commanded with a heavy heart. At the utterance of the word, the Igala joined the fight, adding to the carnage.

The Igala's most feared warriors; the degeli, a bunch especially born and bred to defend the King, ran into the mighty Tiv warriors with their spears cutting them down with such brilliance it rendered their size and strength irrelevant.

The great archers of Ajaka, led by the invincible Chief Omeka, used their bows in near impossibly tight spaces, and when it was too tight for them to fire, they stabbed men to death with their arrows.

The size and might of the Tiv would meet their equal, perhaps slightly greater, against the mighty warriors of Olamaboro. The exchange between the Tiv and the warriors of Olamaboro was a fight between elephants.

The great Chief Ebiloma, the King's most loyal and dear friend. A man who was willing to go to the darkest depths of the underworld for King Idachaba, and his elite; the spear-wielding warriors of Ugwolawo, manoeuvred all over the battle-field matching or beating the powerful swings and thrusts of the Tiv even with the significant difference in their size. The warriors of Ugwolawo spent most of their lives training underwater; the resistance built their swings and thrusts to near-superhuman proportions.

Bassa offered more warriors than any other part of the Kingdom; they came three thousand strong. They ran into the Tiv, wielding their signature short spears, thrusting them into hearts, and bashing men with their shields. The warriors of Ugwolawo, Ajaka, Olamaboro, Bassa, and the other five parts of the Igala kingdom would do their part in the battle. They were exceptional combatants, but even they would know this day that the Tiv were special themselves.

King Terkura circled left and decapitated the first warrior. He spotted another running towards him and another backing him, fighting another man. He pulled the warrior backing him, using him as a shield. The charging warrior thrust his sword into his comrade. King Terkura pushed the now dead man at the charging warrior, ran towards him, and decapitated him too. Terkura engaged and killed two more, walked to an unsuspecting third, and stabbed him in the back. The Tiv King looked around the battle-field, apparently in search of something that was proving difficult to find. With squinted eyes, he scanned the battle-field until his eyes fell on King Okpoju. At the sight of him, the Tor Tiv roared and went on a rampage, fighting his way to the only kill that mattered to him.

King Okpoju was a man of weird quirks and strange antics; he'd kill a man and make statements such as, "Alekwu, this one is on his way," and when a man almost got him he said, "Alekwu, not today, Okpoju must live a while longer." The Idoma King head-butted a man, swept him off his feet, and drove his sword into his heart. He had a long exchange with another but eventually found his heart as well. Standing over the dead warrior's body, he said, "Okpoju was killing men long before your father got between your mother's legs!" The Idoma King turned around and noticed his next opponent, one of the few female warriors on the battle-field. She gave him a savage grin and raised her sword, he walked carefully sideways, grabbed one of his warriors by the arm, and told him, "You fight her. I'll have your man." The Idoma King took his stance in front of his new opponent and said in an inaudible whisper, "Imagine what they'd say if Okpoju lost to a woman. Alekwu forbid, I'm not taking that chance." The Idoma King went on fighting and killing men until he found himself momentarily free of an opponent. He watched some of his men killing, some of them dying, and others giving the Tiv their best effort to stay alive. He watched Igala warriors of Olamaboro and Tiv tussle like elephants, the warriors of Ajaka letting arrows loose like nothing he'd ever seen, he saw the warriors of Ugwolawo thrust their spears into men so fast and hard their weapons went through them, and he also saw the degeli put on the most flawless display of violence he'd ever witnessed. To think that anything could be more impressive than what the King had just witnessed would be impossible if you asked him, but Okpoju's gaze fell on two men fighting back-to-back. One of them was ambidextrous; he wielded two swords and showed remarkable speed as he disarmed men, slit throats, and beat multiple opponents. The other wielded a single sword, his speed was blinding; he was even faster than the other man. Like the other man, he was killing multiple opponents beautifully and with little effort. Okpoju watched the man draw and throw knives at men faster than he'd seen great archers fire arrows. Both men fought as one, they engaged and switched opponents like a choreographed dance. Okpoju stood in awe of the display and his mouth would be agape when both men stood amid six opponents, drew and passed their throwing knives to each other, throwing them, killing all six men and a few more approaching afterward. The King could not believe his eyes, he whispered, "Those two are making children of men." Out of nowhere, a man attacked Okpoju, raining combinations on him. The King blocked his every strike and killed him. He noticed an Igala Captain, Kama of Ugwolawo walking past. King Okpoju stopped him and asked, "Who are those men over there?" pointing at the two men he'd been watching.

"Those are the Princes, Achile and Achimugu, Your Highness," Captain Kama replied, engaging a Tiv warrior immediately after.

"Achile and Achimugu!" he said, particularly surprised. "I knew them when they were little boys."

After killing countless men, Terkura was stood two kills away from his old friend. He swept and struck the first man, walked to the next, blocked a thrust to the head, and tore his belly open with a vicious slicing cut. Two other warriors got between Terkura and Okpoju. After dishing and taking a few hits, the King killed them. The Tor Tiv inhaled and exhaled; calming himself to better enjoy killing the treacherous man he once called brother. Terkura frowned and screamed as he ran towards Okpoju.

Okpoju watched Terkura's every step, he felt sweat run down his forehead, and he felt the rage that brought him to this battle vanish. King Okpoju watched his brother draw close, and raise his sword to strike him. Before this moment, King Okpoju, a battle-tested veteran of many wars would've sworn he'd do otherwise, but the Idoma King threw down his sword and opened his arms, submitting himself to the approaching swing of Terkura's sword. He could not fight him let alone kill him.

King Terkura was only inches away from King Okpoju's head when he was consumed by the same emotions; brotherly love. He stopped himself and turned away, putting his hand over his mouth; he couldn't believe what he was about to do. The Tor Tiv couldn't believe he was a swing of a sword away from killing the best friend he'd ever had. A man he'd come to love more than his blood brothers, a man he'd trusted with his most guarded secrets, and a man who understood him better than any person dead or living. The King lost the battle against his emotions, and the tears came running down his cheeks. With his back still turned to Okpoju he managed to say, "What was I about to do?" he looked around the battle-field, "What have I done?" he said. For whatever strange reason, everything that should have stopped the Tor Tiv from waging war only now dawned on him. It was too late to stop any men from dying now, many lives were already lost. But it wasn't too late to stop the loss of any more lives.

"Stand down!" King Terkura shouted at the top of his voice.

The Captains repeated the King's order, "Stand down!" around the battle-field.

Gradually the fighting stopped. King Terkura faced King Okpoju, and with tears running down both men's cheeks they embraced each other.

"Brother, I support your union. She is yours. I'm sorry, I'm truly sorry," said King Terkura.

"I wronged you. I shouldn't have gone after her. It is I who is sorry," King Okpoju replied.

King Idachaba stood with his battle-axe over his shoulder as he smiled at the sight of the Kings making peace, his smile vanishes, the Igala King looked to the dead bodies littered around, and shook his head as he walked to Akpai.

And so it ended, with thousands of lives lost in the name of a beauty named Iveh. Okpoju reconsidered marrying her, she was the woman that caused the rift between him and his most dear friend, but King Terkura advised against it and convinced him to keep Iveh. That night they toasted to true love, friendship, and mercy from the gods. Kings Okpoju and Terkura were talked about across Kingdoms. The reason for their war was no longer a secret; word of it traveled far and wide. Some spoke their names to exemplify shameful behavior, especially, regarding lust and attraction. The storytellers and comedians mocked them in market squares. People gathered in public places thrashing their names. Word of it was often brought to them by their messengers, and both Kings took it all without ordering men beaten or punished in any way; they felt it was well deserved. For many years the Kings had done most things together, feasting, fighting, chasing women, and now the embarrassment they felt from all that happened weighed lighter because now more than ever, they knew they had each other and they would face the shame like they did everything else; together. Both Kings believed the experience was a curse from the gods. They accepted it, learnt from it, and their bond grew stronger because of it.

About the Author

C.E. Ocheja is a writer and author of fiction. A graduate with a BSc in Business Management with a passion for storytelling. When Ocheja isn't writing, he trains in combat sports, plays chess, watches combat sports, American football, basketball, gymnastics, listens to a lot of music, appreciates the Opera, Cirque du Soleil, and the ballet.

You can connect with me on:
- https://www.talkingdrumwriting.com
- https://web.facebook.com/Mr.Ocheja
- https://web.facebook.com/TalkingDrumWriting
- https://www.instagram.com/c.e.ocheja

Subscribe to my newsletter:
- https://www.talkingdrumwriting.com

Also by Christopher Ocheja

The next short story is scheduled to be released soon. Follow us on all platforms to stay informed. The events of this book take place during the "Nine Long Years" period of the main title.

AKUMABI'S FIRST KILL

Are killers born, or are they bred? Does killing come naturally to man, or are we nurtured directly or indirectly by experience?

There is a killer in every man, asleep, but make no mistake, he can be awoken by a desperate need to survive.